The Night Before Christmas

The Night before Christmas or a Visit of St Nicholas

CLEMENT CLARKE MOORE

AN ANTIQUE REPRODUCTION

PHILOMEL BOOKS

NEW YORK

INTRODUCTION

BIBLICAL scholars generally agree that the original Saint Nicholas was a fourth century Byzantine bishop who was associated with gift giving and the protection of children. He was known for his fierce defense of the Christian faith and was depicted in early Greek icons as tall and thin. That image of him continued beyond the Protestant Reformation. Then, when saints were no longer venerated by non-Catholics, St. Nicholas was transformed into the willowy figures of Father Christmas in England, Père Nöel in France, Weinachtsman in Germany, and Sinter Klaas in Holland. The jolly, rotund Santa Claus the world knows today was a nineteenth century American invention that almost went unnoticed.

"A Visit of St. Nicholas," a poem better known to most of us by its first line, "T'was the night before Christmas," was written by Clement Clarke Moore on Christmas Eve, 1822, as a gift for his children. Dr. Moore was the son of New York's second Episcopal Bishop, the Rt. Rev. Benjamin Moore, and served as a professor of bible studies and Greek and Hebrew at General Theological Seminary in New York City. Moore based his poem on a Dutch legend he had remembered from his boyhood, but his Santa Claus was completely his own invention. At his boyhood home in Chelsea, there had been a Dutch caretaker by the name of Jan Duyckinck, who was fat, jolly, bewhiskered and smoked a pipe. Moore used his boyhood memory of that groundskeeper to transform Santa Claus into a jolly old elf with a little round belly and a beard as white as snow who smoked a stump of a pipe. Why Moore changed Father Christmas' horse into eight tiny reindeer remains a mystery.

Moore never intended that "A Visit of St. Nicholas" be published. But a family friend copied the poem and sent it without Moore's knowledge to the *Troy* (New York) *Sentinel,* where it was first published anonymously on December 23, 1823. Had it not been for this unauthorized publication, the poem might never have become part of our Christmas tradition, and the catalyst to transform Santa Claus into a jovial, fur-trimmed gift giver who slips down chimneys to spread Christmas cheer. As it happened, the poem became an instant success and was reprinted throughout the Christian world. Thomas Nast, America's foremost political cartoonist of the nineteenth century, used Moore's description of St. Nicholas as the basis for many drawings of Santa Claus that permanently set the image we all know and love today. It wasn't until many years after he had written the poem, however, that Moore finally admitted his authorship, wanting instead to be remembered for his more scholarly works.

This edition of "A Visit of St. Nicholas" is a faithful reproduction of an 1888 McLoughlin Bros. publication of the Moore poem, which is considered by some scholars to be the first example of children's verse written with no moral instruction. The illustrations are by William Roger Snow (1834–1907) who drew for McLoughlin Bros. under the pseudonym of Richard Andre to avoid legal problems in his native England. It is republished here with the hope that Clement Clarke Moore's words and the beautiful pictures they conjure up will continue to delight many future generations.

Dr. Russell Barber

"THE NIGHT BEFORE CHRISTMAS."

"ALL SNUG IN THEIR BEDS."

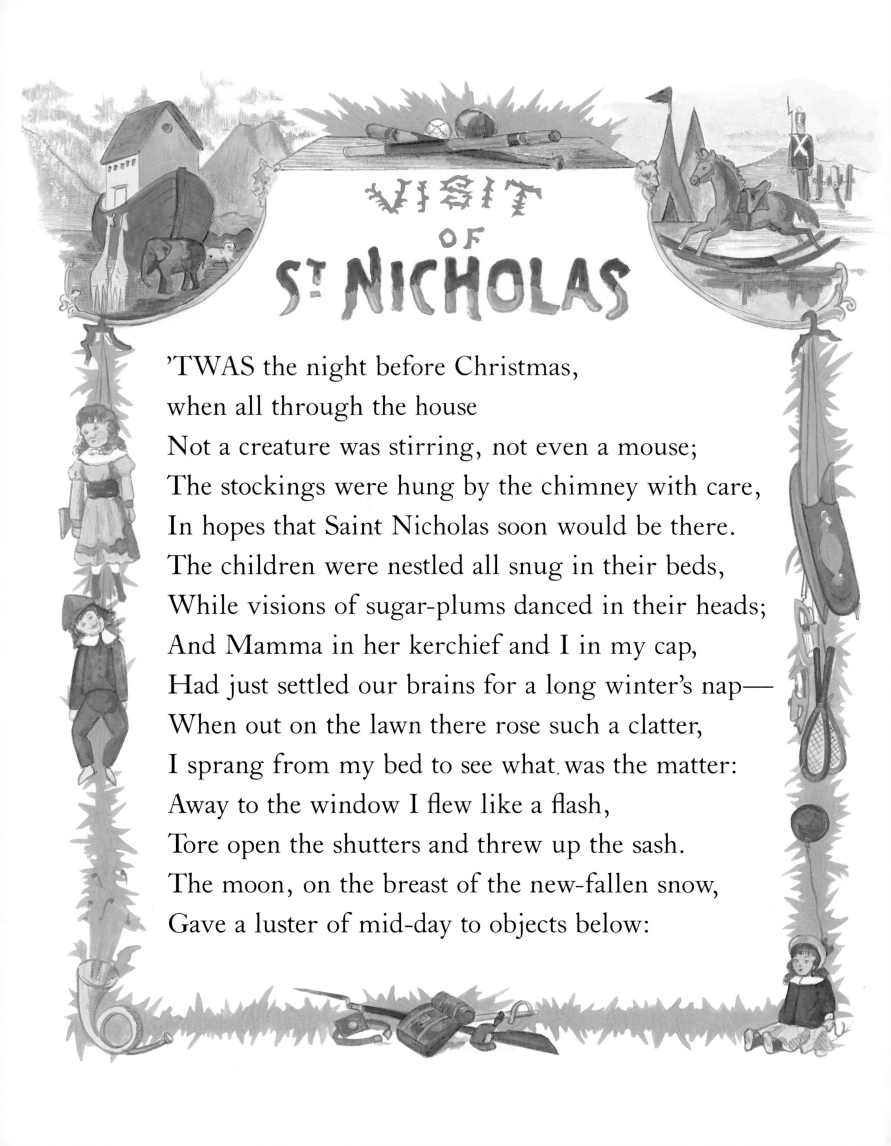

VISIT
OF
St NICHOLAS

'TWAS the night before Christmas,
when all through the house
Not a creature was stirring, not even a mouse;
The stockings were hung by the chimney with care,
In hopes that Saint Nicholas soon would be there.
The children were nestled all snug in their beds,
While visions of sugar-plums danced in their heads;
And Mamma in her kerchief and I in my cap,
Had just settled our brains for a long winter's nap—
When out on the lawn there rose such a clatter,
I sprang from my bed to see what was the matter:
Away to the window I flew like a flash,
Tore open the shutters and threw up the sash.
The moon, on the breast of the new-fallen snow,
Gave a luster of mid-day to objects below:

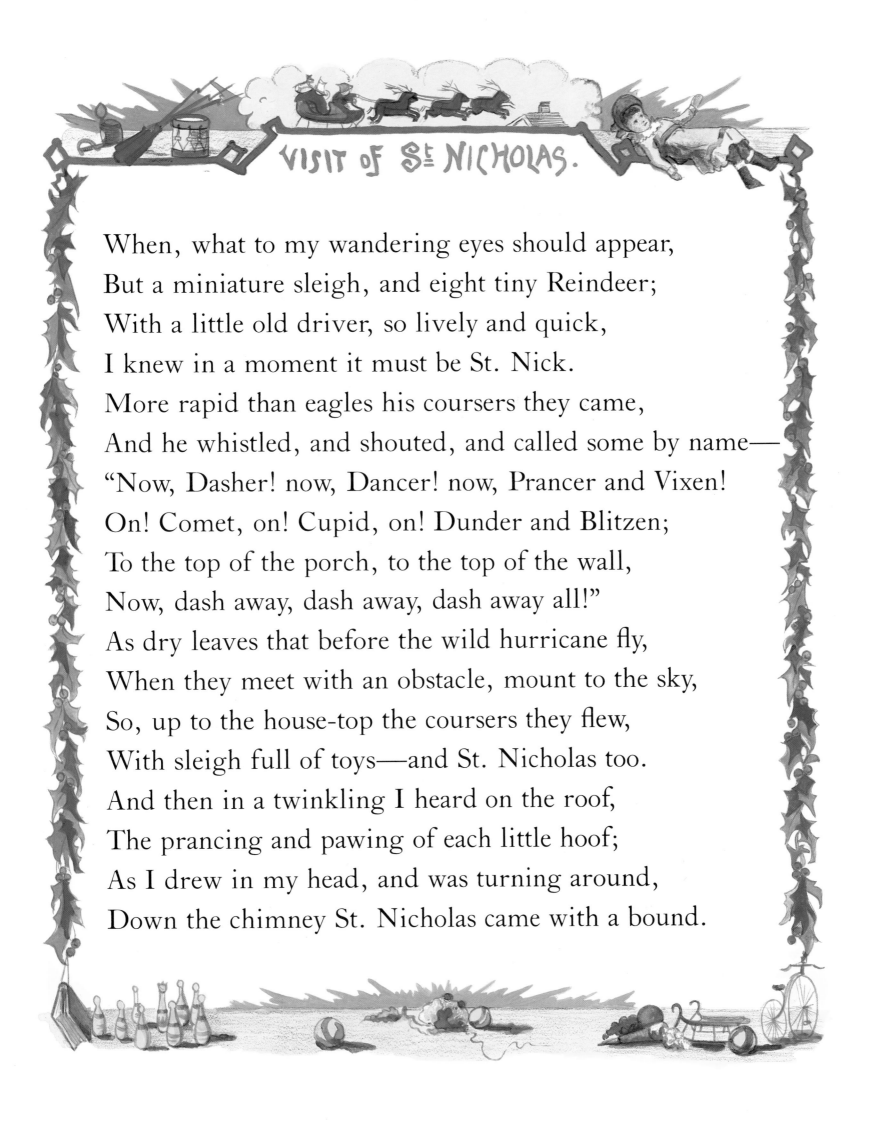

VISIT OF St. NICHOLAS.

When, what to my wandering eyes should appear,
But a miniature sleigh, and eight tiny Reindeer;
With a little old driver, so lively and quick,
I knew in a moment it must be St. Nick.
More rapid than eagles his coursers they came,
And he whistled, and shouted, and called some by name—
"Now, Dasher! now, Dancer! now, Prancer and Vixen!
On! Comet, on! Cupid, on! Dunder and Blitzen;
To the top of the porch, to the top of the wall,
Now, dash away, dash away, dash away all!"
As dry leaves that before the wild hurricane fly,
When they meet with an obstacle, mount to the sky,
So, up to the house-top the coursers they flew,
With sleigh full of toys—and St. Nicholas too.
And then in a twinkling I heard on the roof,
The prancing and pawing of each little hoof;
As I drew in my head, and was turning around,
Down the chimney St. Nicholas came with a bound.

"A MINIATURE SLEIGH, AND EIGHT TINY REINDEER."

"DOWN THE CHIMNEY ST. NICHOLAS CAME."

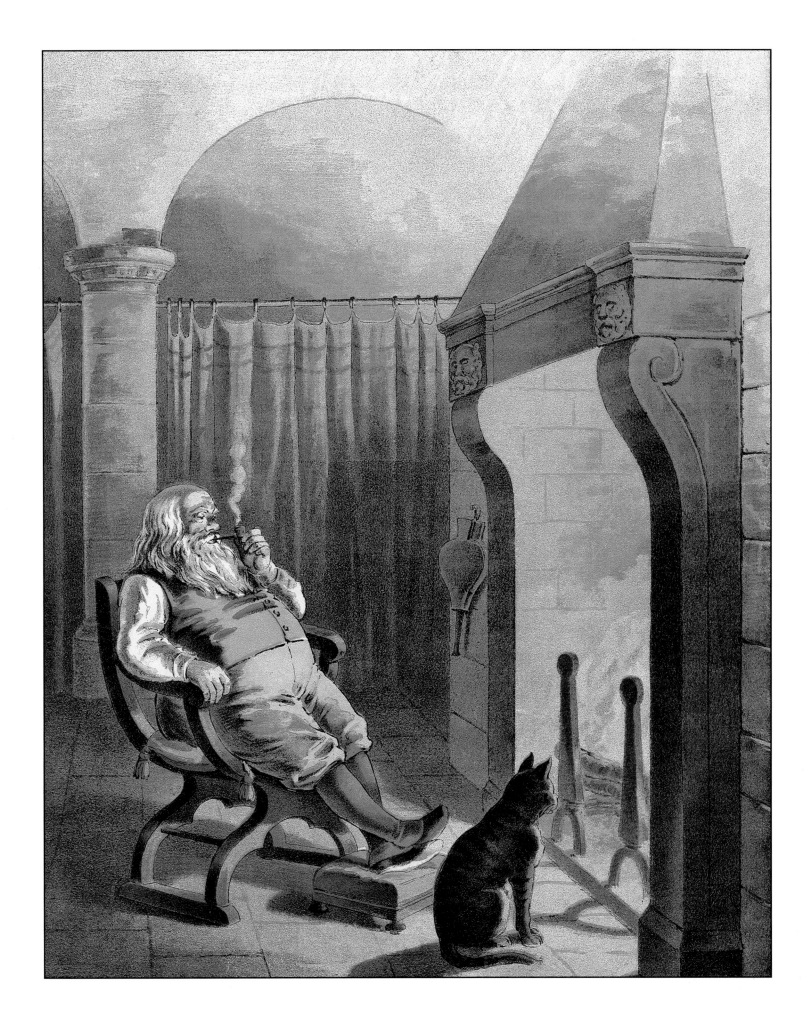

"AND HE WHISTLED, AND SHOUTED, AND CALLED SOME BY
NAME—NOW, DASHER! NOW, DANCER!

NOW, PRANCER AND VIXEN! ON! COMET, ON! CUPID, ON!
DUNDER AND BLITZEN."

He was dressed all in fur
From his head to his foot,
And his clothes were all tarnished
With ashes and soot:
A bundle of toys
He had flung on his back,
And he looked like a peddler
Just opening his pack;
His eyes how they twinkled!
His dimples how merry—
His cheeks were like roses,
His nose like a cherry;
His droll little mouth
Was drawn up like a bow,
And the beard on his chin
Was as white as the snow.
The stump of a pipe
He held tight in his teeth,
And the smoke, it encircled
His head like a wreath.
He had a broad face
And a little round belly
That shook when he laughed,
Like a bowl-full of jelly.

"HE LOOKED LIKE A PEDDLER JUST OPENING HIS PACK."

"HIS EYES HOW THEY TWINKLED! HIS DIMPLES HOW MERRY!"

He was chubby and plump—
  A right jolly old elf;
And I laughed when I saw him
  In spite of myself.
A wink of his eye,
  And a twist of his head,
Soon gave me to know
  I had nothing to dread.
He spoke not a word,
  But went straight to his work,
And filled all the stockings:
  Then turned with a jerk,
And laying his finger
  Aside of his nose,
And giving a nod,
  Up the chimney he rose.
He sprang to his sleigh,
  To his team gave a whistle,
And away they all flew
  Like the down of a thistle:
But I heard him exclaim
  Ere he drove out of sight,
"MERRY CHRISTMAS TO ALL,
  AND TO ALL A GOOD NIGHT."

"AND FILLED ALL THE STOCKINGS."

"MERRY CHRISTMAS TO ALL AND TO ALL A GOOD NIGHT."

This Philomel edition is a faithful reproduction of an antique book originally published circa 1870. The artwork, created from stone lithographs, and the text appear in their original order, with the exception of the frontispiece which appeared on the back cover in the original edition. The introduction, title and colophon pages have been added, and decorated with delicate watercolor border illustrations imitating the border illustrations of inside pages. All borders, both new and replicated, have been hand-painted by Carol Endler Sterbenz.

This book was brought to Philomel by Russell Barber, Religion Editor at WNBC Television in New York. He studied at The University of Puget Sound in Tacoma, Washington, and received a master's in speech from Stanford University and a PhD. in communication from Northwestern University.

Introduction copyright © 1989 by Enlightenment Enterprises Inc.
Published by Philomel Books, a division of The Putnam & Grosset Group,
200 Madison Avenue, New York, NY 10016.
All rights reserved. Published simultaneously in Canada.
Printed in Hong Kong by South China Printing Co. (1988) Ltd.
Book design by Christy Hale
First Philomel Edition 1989
Third Impression.
Library of Congress Cataloging-in-Publication Data
Moore, Clement Clarke, 1779-1863.
The night before Christmas or a visit of St. Nicholas/by Clement Clarke Moore. p. cm.
Summary: The well-known poem about an important Christmas Eve visitor.
1. Santa Claus—Juvenile Poetry.   2. Christmas—Juvenile poetry.
3. Children's poetry, American. [1. Santa Claus—Poetry.
2. Christmas—Poetry.   3. American poetry.   4. Narrative poetry.]
I. Title.   II. Title: Visit of St. Nicholas.
PS2429.M5N5 1989 811'.2—dc19 88-19600 CIP AC
ISBN 0-399-21614-6